PETER'S DREAM

STORY
JOAN HOFFMAN

ILLUSTRATIONS
JOYCE JOHN

Peter has a new boat.
Now he can sail the seas.

He can sail to far-off lands
where he has no one to please.

He dreamed he sailed to places
where pirates sailed before.

He looked for lost treasures
on the ocean floor.

Sea animals did not scare him.
They all became his friends.

They led him to a strange land
where no one had ever been.

This land is in another world.
No one lives there but girls and boys.

There is no one there to tell them they must share their toys.

There is no one to tell them when and what to eat.

There is no one to tell them
when to go to sleep.

No one is there to tell them
the right things to wear.

And if they get all dirty,
no one really cares.

No one is there to help them
when there is a fight.

No one is there to hug them
and make everything all right.

And when they have a bad dream, there is no one to turn on the light. MOM!